Hello, Reader!

Purple bloomers, purple bloomers,
Oh, how you shine and glow.
Purple bloomers, purple bloomers,
I'll never let you go!

Join Mother Koala, Harry, and Matilda on the funniest shopping trip ever!

To Pam

Originally published in 1992 in England by
André Deutsch Children's Books, an imprint of Scholastic
Publications Limited.

Text copyright © 1992 by Ronda Armitage.
Illustrations copyright © 1992 by David Armitage.
All rights reserved. Published by Scholastic Inc.,
730 Broadway, New York, NY 10003, by arrangement with
André Deutsch Children's Books, an imprint of
Scholastic Publications Limited.
CARTWHEEL BOOKS is a trademark of Scholastic Inc.
HELLO READER! is a registered trademark of Scholastic Inc.

LIBRARY OF CONGRESS CATALOGING-IN-PUBLICATION DATA

Armitage, Ronda.
  Harry hates shopping! / Ronda and David Armitage.
     p.   cm. — (Hello reader)
  Summary: Mother Koala must get the upper hand when her two
children Harry and Matilda quarrel during a shopping trip.
  ISBN 0-590-90746-8
  [1. Koala—Fiction.   2. Brothers and sisters—Fiction.
3. Behavior—Fiction.   4. Shopping—Fiction.]   I. Armitage, David.
1943-   ill. II. Title. III. Series.
PZ7.A73Har   1992
[E]—dc20   92-27945
                                                        CIP
                                                        AC

12 11 10   7 8/9

HARRY
HATES
SHOPPING!

Ronda and David Armitage

Cartwheel
·B·O·O·K·S· ®
SCHOLASTIC INC.
New York   Toronto   London   Auckland   Sydney

"We're going shopping today," Mother Koala
announced at breakfast.

She smiled at Harry and Matilda.

"I don't want to go shopping," growled Harry.
"I hate shopping."

"I don't," said Matilda. "I just love it. I'm going to buy some new boots. Red ones with plaid laces and furry insides."

"I'm not sure about red, dear," said Mother.
"They might not have red. A nice brown would be
more sensible. Koalas look very stylish in brown.
I'm sorry about the shopping, Harry, but you
really do need new school shoes."

"No, I don't," protested Harry. "There's nothing wrong with my old white sneakers. They're fine."

Mother Koala sighed. "If you're both very good, we'll have lunch out after we're done shopping."

Matilda danced along the sidewalk.

Harry trudged behind.

Suddenly Matilda fell over.

"Mom!" she wailed. "Harry tripped me. He stuck out his foot and tripped me."

"Harry," said Mother, "what's the matter with you? Do you have to be such a pain?"

"Matilda is being a pest," said Harry. "All that skipping and dancing. She's such a show-off."

Mother sighed.

First they went to the drugstore. Matilda
pinched Harry while Mother was buying
toothpaste.

"Mom!" Harry yelled.

Next they went to the bakery. Harry pinched
Matilda while Mother was buying rolls.
"Mom!" Matilda cried loudly.

Mother marched Harry and Matilda outside.
"If you two don't stop arguing," she growled,
"I'm going to get really angry."

At last they reached the department store.
"One more word out of either of you," said
Mother, "and I don't know *what* I might do."

While Mother was looking at some new
T-shirts, Harry stuck his tongue out at Matilda.

"*Mother!*" wailed Matilda, "Harry's being
horrible again. He's making faces at me!"
And then she stopped and stared at her mother.

Mother Koala had picked up a pair of very large
purple bloomers. They were all shiny with big
pink spots and squiggles on them.

She held them up in front of her and began to
sing in a loud, tuneful voice.

Purple bloomers, purple bloomers,
Oh, how you shine and glow.
Purple bloomers, purple bloomers,
I'll never let you go!

Harry turned bright red and dived under
a chair.

"Mom," hissed Harry. "Stop that! Everybody's
looking. Please, stop."

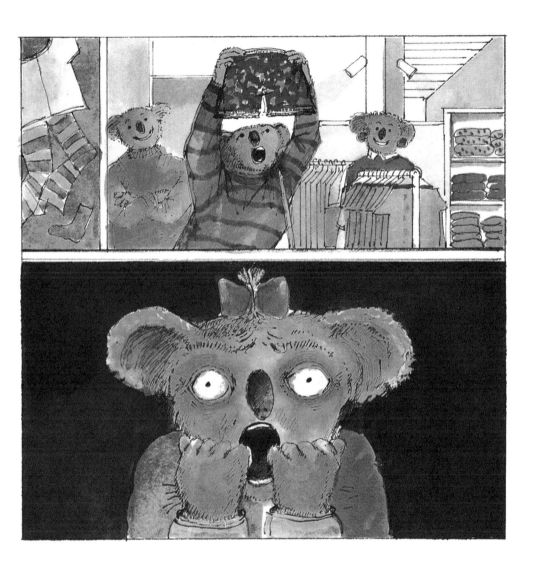

Matilda's eyes opened wide. She hid behind
the counter.

Mother Koala went right on singing. And while
she sang, she danced.

"Psst, Mom," whispered Matilda, "you're
embarrassing us. Please, stop."

Mother smiled at Matilda and waved at Harry.
"I'll take these purple bloomers," she said to the
salesperson. "How much are they?"

"Now, children," said Mother, "it's time to buy shoes."

Harry and Matilda crept out of their hiding places. They didn't say a word.

"That was fun," said Mother. "I've always enjoyed singing."

The shoe store didn't have red boots. The salesman suggested a bright green pair instead.

"I don't want those," said Matilda. "They don't have plaid laces and furry insides."

Harry found a pair of boots that he really liked. "I'm sorry, young man," said the salesman, "but we don't have those in your size. How about this nice brown pair?"

"I don't like those," growled Harry.
Matilda looked as if she were going to cry.

Very slowly Mother opened her package. Very
carefully she unwrapped the tissue paper. Very
quietly she began to sing.

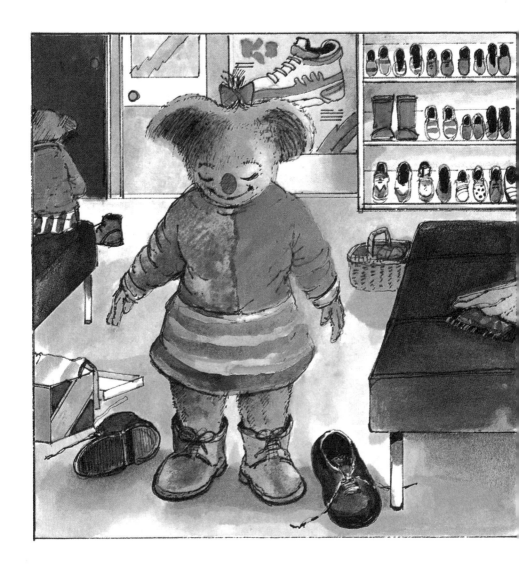

"I think maybe I do like these green boots after all," said Matilda. "Actually, I think they're very nice boots."

She tied up the laces.

"Yes," said Harry quickly. "I'll try on the brown boots. They'll be very, very nice for school."

"I agree," said Mother as she paid the bill. "They are very, very, very nice boots."

They had a delicious lunch in the coffee shop at
the top of the store.

Matilda smiled at Harry. Harry smiled at
Matilda.

"What lovely children I have," said Mother Koala.
And she smiled happily at both of them.